A Mountain of Mittens

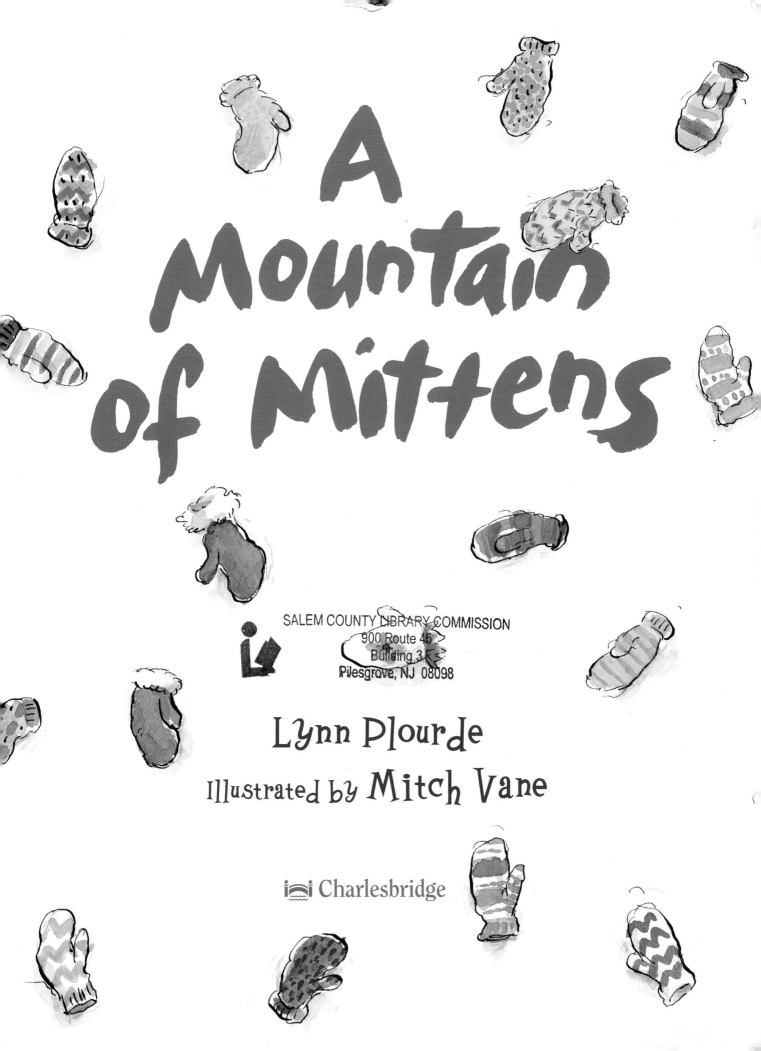

A Mountain of Mittens

Lynn Plourde

Illustrated by Mitch Vane

Charlesbridge

A mountain of thanks to Sue Cohen
—L. P.

For the snow bunnies: Matt, Tani, Natasha, Dexter, and Spencer
—M. V.

2009 First paperback edition
Text copyright © 2007 by Lynn Plourde
Illustrations copyright © 2007 by Mitch Vane

Published by Charlesbridge
85 Main Street
Watertown, MA 02472
(617) 926-0329
www.charlesbridge.com

Library of Congress Cataloging-in-Publication Data
Plourde, Lynn.
    A mountain of mittens / Lynn Plourde ; illustrated by Mitch Vane.
       p. cm.
    Summary: Molly's parents try various methods to help her
remember her mittens but nothing seems to work.
ISBN 978-1-57091-585-7 (reinforced for library use)
ISBN 978-1-57091-466-9 (softcover)
    [1. Mittens—Fiction. 2. Lost and found possessions—Fiction.]
I. Vane, Mitch, ill. II. Title.
    PZ7.P724Mou 2007
    [E]—dc22   2006021253

Printed in China
(hc) 10 9 8 7 6 5 4 3 2
(sc) 10 9 8 7 6 5 4 3 2 1

Illustrations done in watercolor and dip pen and India ink
    on Arches watercolor paper
Display type and text type set in Flora Dora and Berkeley,
    hand-lettering by Mitch Vane
Color separations by Chroma Graphics, Singapore
Printed and bound by Regent Publishing Services
Production supervision by Brian G. Walker
Designed by Diane M. Earley

It was that time of year again.

"Don't forget your mittens at school!" yelled Molly's parents.

"Nope, I won't," answered Molly.

Molly still had her mittens during morning recess, during lunch recess, and during afternoon recess. But just as she put on her mittens to leave school at the end of the day, she heard a teensy, weensy sneeze—achoo! There shivering and quivering in a corner of the terrarium was the class turtle, Myrtle. Achoo—achoo!

"Oh, bless you, bless you, Myrtle Turtle. You must be catching a cold," said Molly. "Here, cuddle in my mittens. They'll keep you cozy."

After school Molly's teacher, Mr. Jolly, discovered
Molly's mittens, along with a few other mittens. He put
them in the lost-and-found pile and mumbled, "They
forgot their mittens."

Mittens, Mittens.

My, oh, my!

A Mountain of Mittens,
Piled up
high.

LOST AND FOUND

The next day Molly's parents Velcro-ed Molly's mittens to her jacket. So did the other kids' parents.

"Don't forget your mittens at school!" yelled Molly's parents.

"Nope, I won't. No way," answered Molly.

Molly still had her mittens during morning recess, during lunch recess, and during afternoon recess. But at the end of the day, Molly and her whole grade practiced their winter musical on stage with Miss Holly, the music teacher.

Miss Holly played the piano with her fingers and jingled bells with her toes as Molly and all the other students fa-la-la-ed in their winter clothes. They even practiced opening and closing the stage curtains and taking a bow.

After school Miss Holly discovered Molly's mittens, along with a few other mittens. She put them in the lost-and-found pile and mumbled and grumbled, "They forgot their mittens!"

Mittens, mittens.
my, oh, my!

A Mountain of Mittens,
piled
up
high.

The next day Molly's parents crocheted her mittens together with a chain of yarn. So did the other kids' parents.

"Don't forget your mittens at school!" yelled Molly's parents.

"Nope, I won't. No way, no how," answered Molly.

Molly still had her mittens during morning recess, during lunch recess, and during afternoon recess. But just as Molly put on her mittens at the end of the day for the ride home, Mr. Golly's bus went slippery-slide-sloosh and slid off the snowy road.

"Oh golly, Mr. Golly," said Molly. "Don't worry. We'll help." Molly and the other students used the yarn chains on their mittens to lasso, yank, tug, and pull the bus back onto the road.

After all the students were safely bused home, Mr. Golly discovered Molly's mittens, along with a few other mittens. He drove back to the school, put them in the lost-and-found pile, and mumbled and grumbled and rumbled, "THEY FORGOT THEIR MITTENS!"

Mittens,
Mittens.

My, oh, my!
A
Mountain
of
Mittens,

Piled
up
high.

The next day Molly's
parents duct-taped Molly's
mittens to her jacket. So did
the other kids' parents.

"Don't forget your mittens at
school!" yelled Molly's parents.
"Nope, I won't. No way, no
how. Not me," answered Molly.

Molly still had her mittens during morning recess, during lunch recess, and during afternoon recess. But at the end of the day, just as Molly put on her mittens, the principal, Mrs. Folly, called an emergency assembly.

Mrs. Folly announced into the microphone, "No one, I repeat no one, will be allowed to leave school today until you all reclaim your mittens from the lost-and-found pile."

"Yikes!" said Molly. "The bus is waiting."
So she dove into the lost-and-found pile,
along with a few other students.

GRIP STICK STUCK!

Molly and the other students were
duct-taped to the pile.

"Holy mittens!" yelled Mrs. Folly. "We can't have our students stuck at school overnight." So Mrs. Folly hollered, "HE-E-E-E-E-ELP!"

Then Mr. Jolly, Miss Holly, Mr. Golly, and Mrs. Folly tussled and tugged to try to free Molly and the other students.

They got stuck, too.

Molly, Mr. Jolly,
Miss Holly,
Mr. Golly,
Mrs. Folly,
and more.

My, oh, my!
A Mountain
of people,
Piled
up
High.

Meanwhile Molly's parents paced and fretted,
"Where, oh where, is Molly? We're worried—she's
late." When they called the school and got no
answer, they quickly dialed 9-1-1.

Then Molly's parents raced to school,
along with a few other parents . . .
and police officers . . .
and firefighters . . .
and ambulance workers.

With special snip-snapping cutting equipment and super-duper teamwork, everyone was freed from the duct tape in no time flat.

"Hooray!" yelled Molly, along with a few other students.

"Hooray!" yelled Molly's parents, along with a few other parents.

Everyone high-fived and hurried home for supper.
Everyone, that is, except Mr. Jolly, Miss Holly,
Mr. Golly, and Mrs. Folly. They mumbled and grumbled
and rumbled and roared,

Mittens,
Mittens.
My, oh, my!
A
Mountain
of
Mittens,
Piled
up
high.